This Big Talkabout book is full of attractive, colourful and interesting pictures which will provide hours of enjoyment for your child. We know that the early growth of language and an ever widening vocabulary are very important for a young child and this book has been specially planned to cover most of the areas which will be helpful to your child before he or she goes to school.

You will help your child by using the pages in this book for talking with him or her. On each page, a short question or title has been given to help you. There are no particular answers to most of the questions because it is more important that your child should just talk about the pictures. By talking with him you can help him relate the pictures to the things he knows from his own experience. For example, in the section called 'Have you heard these?' – first you might ask the child what is the name of each of these things which makes a noise. Then show him how clapping hands make a sound, and let him do it with you. Can he remember the noise the vacuum cleaner makes when you are cleaning? What other things make different sounds? You could talk about the sound of the cars and lorries passing by outside. Most children these days recognise the sound of a police car or fire engine siren. What about things which only make a little noise? Let your child talk about the sounds he can make, like splashing in the bath, knocking at the door and creeping up the stairs without making a sound.

On the last page there are some further suggestions on how you can extend the use of this picture book with games and activities which your child will enjoy.

Acknowledgment:
The photographs and endpapers are by Hurlston Design Ltd.

0 7214 7504 3

my first big talkabout book

with illustrations by
Harry Wingfield, Martin Aitchison and Eric Winter

LADYBIRD BOOKS LOUGHBOROUGH 1978

fun with colour

Which colours are the same?

Talk about the colours

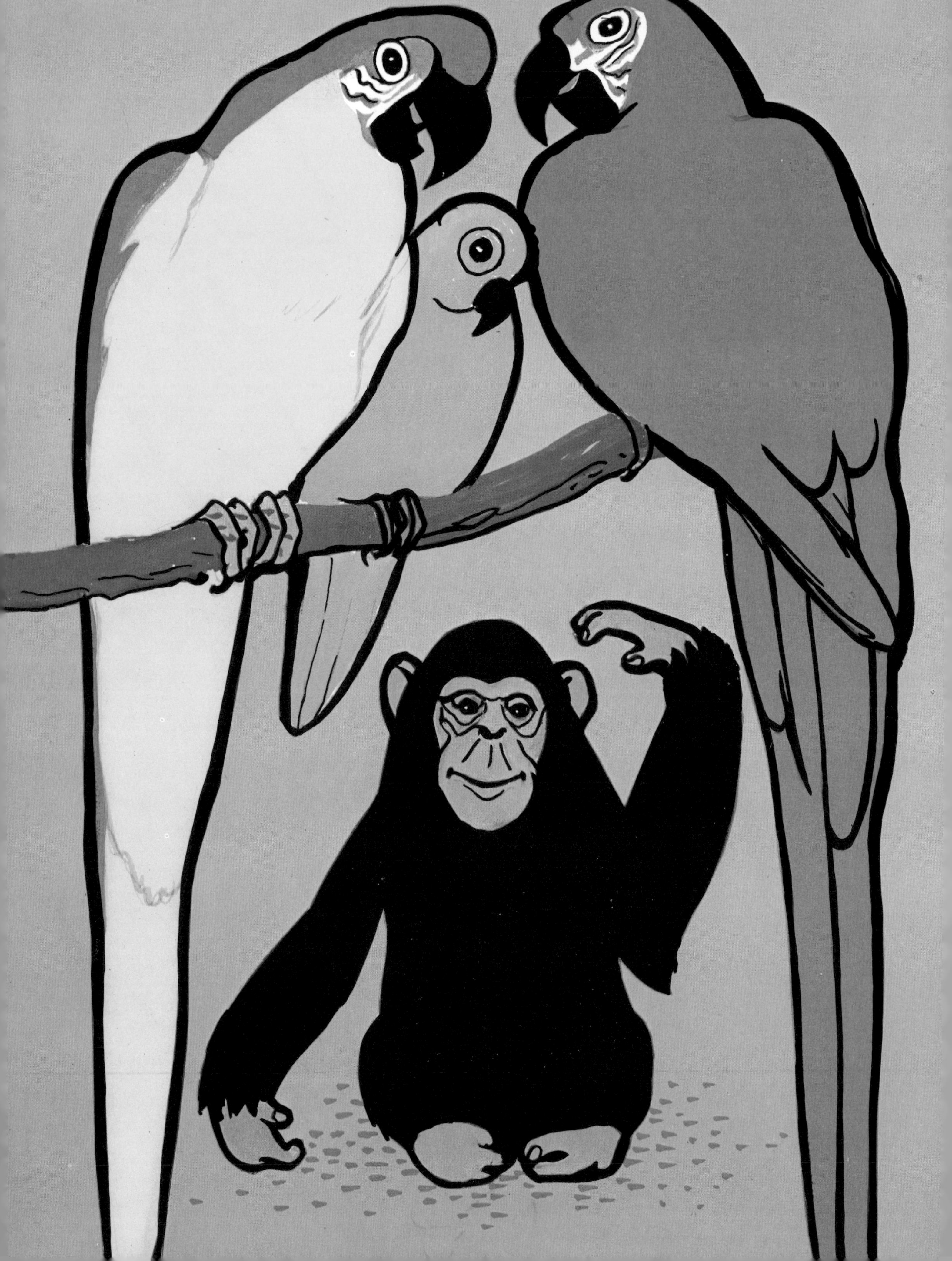

look and find

Where does each
piece fit?

**Find one
the same
as this**

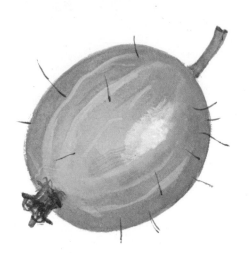

. . . and this

. . . and this

. . . and this

Match the picture
with the shape

Which shop sells these?

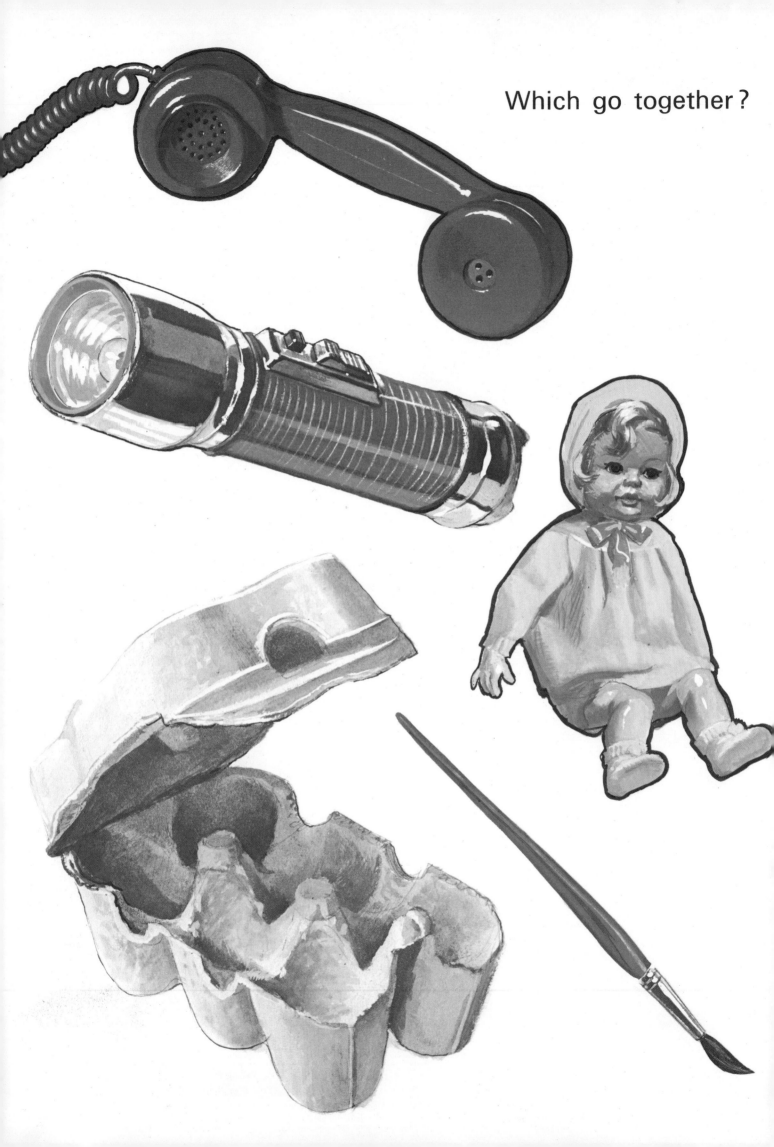

Which go together?

using your senses

Have you **felt** these?

Have you **seen** these?

What noise does each animal make?

Have you **tasted** these?

Have you **heard** these?

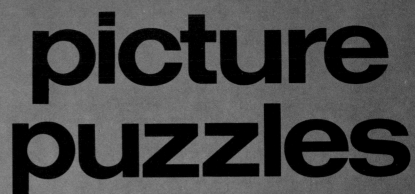

picture puzzles

Who catches the fish?

and can you name each colour?

Who owns which dog?

looking at nature

Can you name these animals and birds?

Rabbit

Fish

Guinea Pig

Gerbil

Cat

What are
these pets called?

Talk about the hungry birds

What is in the garden?

What is above and below the ground?

Spring

Summer

Autumn

Winter

Talk about the whole year

tell me a story

1

2

3

4

Who gets wet?

Tell the 'long dog' story

What happens in this story?

Do you know the story of The Three Little Pigs?

The early worm catches the bird

Who wins the race?

What is happening?

A fisherman's story

Tell the story of the bird-table

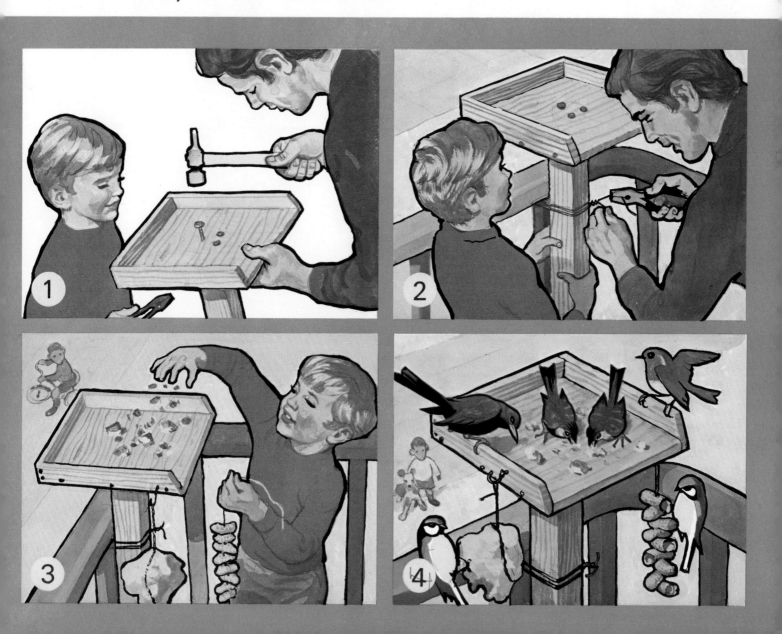

opposites

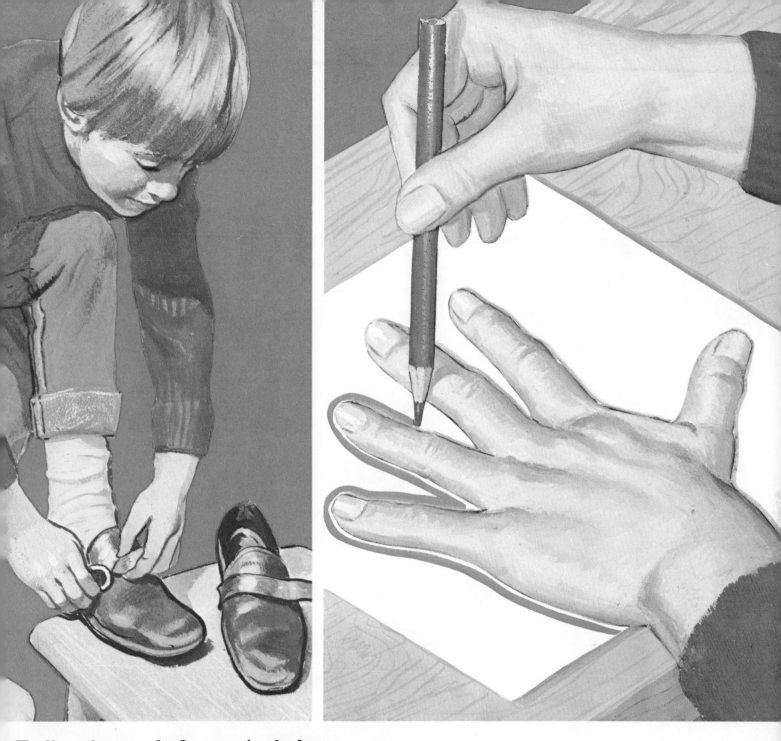

Talk about **left** and **right**

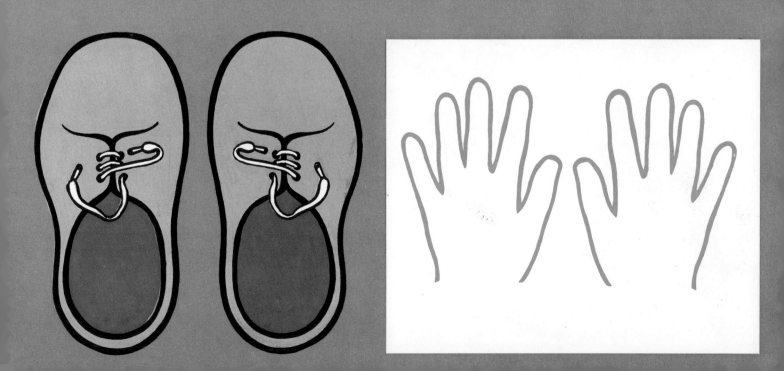

Talk about **big** and **little**

learn to count

1

2

3

4

5

How many eggs?

Count the buttons

1  2

3 4

5  6

Find another number like this 4

2 1 4

. . . and this

3 5 8 3

. . . and this

6 9 6 7

. . . and this

2 1 2 5

How old are you? Can you point to the number?

Count round the clock

What time is it?

You can make this clock

Cut out and stick onto card.
With the little hand on top, attach hands
using a paper fastener through the holes

little hand

big hand

More things to do

Here are a few suggestions for extending the use of each section in this book, after you have talked about the pictures.

Fun with Colour

Does the child know the names of the colours? Can he match the colours in the book with his toys, clothes or things around the home? Provide scrap paper, paints or crayons for him to experiment with colours.

Look and Find

Can your child recognise the shapes around him (e.g. doors, windows, etc.)? Let him handle and play with solid shapes: e.g. boxes, cartons, tubes, etc. Make a set of 'Snap' cards using shapes and colours and play a game with them. Give him simple jigsaws to do.

Senses

Your child may not have heard, seen, tasted, etc., all the things in the pictures, so talk about his own experiences. Does he know the names of animals? Play 'I SPY'. Put small toys in a cloth bag, and play a 'What can you feel?' game.

Puzzles

Make up stories about the pictures, as well as doing the puzzles. Make other puzzle games like 'What's missing?' You lay out a few toys or objects, the child covers his eyes, then you take one of the objects away.